Ellie Juneman: Earth Witch

(in training)

Written by
Rebecca Burke

Illustrated by
Chris Burke

REBECCA BURKE — Author

Though Rebecca's background is based in science, having studied Sports Therapy and worked with the young physically disabled, she has always had a very big imagination and love for faery folklore and nature. Her first children's book, *Bryony Fairview: Weather Witch*, was published in 2020 and she caught the writing bug big time — starting the second book almost immediately! *Ellie Juneman: Earth Witch (in training)* covers the importance of being kind to the world around us and focuses on the power or our own words. Being a mother of two very active, magical children, she has a constant source of inspiration and loves to be able to share this journey with them. Join them in exploring her magical worlds!

CHRIS BURKE — Illustrator

After a lifetime of service, initially in the Defence Forces and then in the Civil Service, Chris discovered his creative side in retirement. His artwork had been displayed in several exhibitions before he turned to illustrating his first children's book, *Bryony Fairview: Weather Witch*, and he was very happy to be able to illustrate the second in the series *Ellie Juneman: Earth Witch (in training)*. He is a grandfather of six and has thoroughly enjoyed channelling the magic of his grandchildren into the illustrations for these books.

First published in 2021 by Child's Eye,
Redshank Books

ISBN 978-1-912969-33-3

A CIP catalogue record for this book is available from The British Library

Cover and design by Carnegie Book Production

Printed in the UK by Halstan

Redshank Books
Brunel House
Volunteer Way
Faringdon
Oxfordshire
SN7 7YR

Tel: +44 (0)845 873 3837

www.libripublishing.co.uk

A special *go raibh maith agat* to the
Cogan-Kenntofts for all their help!

Rebecca Burke, Author

Dedicated to my Grandchildren
Who have made my life more interesting every day!

Chris Burke, Illustrator

'... Bryony started to get her broom ready.

"Before you take Ellie back, I'd like to show her something," Elodie said and led Ellie into the old weather station, stepping through the large crack in the heavy oak door. She walked straight up to the list of names Ellie had noticed on the wall when she had first entered the emerald-roofed building. "These," Elodie explained whilst removing the list from the wall, "are potential Earth Witches that may still be able to practise, or are indeed still practising. I would get small snippets every now and then, but with the storms there was always doubt as to what actually was coming through the radio phone. Now it's smashed, I think you may have more luck finding any surviving Earth Witches in your land. Would you do that for me?" Elodie asked hopefully.

"Of course!" Ellie said excitedly taking the list from Elodie, folding it neatly and placing it safely in her pocket...'

Bryony Fairview: Weather Witch
Written by Rebecca Burke

Contents

Chapter 1

The Bird and the Note

Ellie was an Earth Witch, well an Earth Witch in training that is. She was one of the last known Earth Witches and had been given the task of locating any others that were possibly still around. She had been given a list of names and was sat, cross legged, on her bed with the list on her lap. Ellie looked down at the piece of paper and studied the names that hadn't been crossed out. She felt at a loss — how was she going to find these remaining Earth Witches, if in fact, there were any still practising? As she read and re-read the names she felt a faint pulse pass through her and the acorn necklace around her neck began to glow. Ellie was still learning the Earth Witch trade and had yet to get used to all the sides of her magic. She held the acorn loosely in her hand and then heard a quiet voice saying, 'Look up.'

Ellie glanced around her room. There was a clatter at the window that made her jump off the bed. Outside her window was, what looked like, a blackbird — but not your average blackbird — there was something very different about this one. Suddenly she heard it clearly chirp, 'Look up! Let me in!'

Without a second thought Ellie opened her window and let the bird in. (Since finding a Weather Witch called Bryony in her garden and discovering a whole colourful land behind the clouds last year, Ellie was rarely shocked by the extraordinary.) In flew the bird and it perched on her desk, lifting its claw to reveal that it had a note attached to it. Ellie carefully took the scroll of paper. It read,

'Hello fellow Earth Witch — we have found you at last. We have felt you and seen your power. I am requesting a gathering in the South of all the known remaining Earth Witches, please come. From Georgie Dove.'

A gathering of Earth witches — *all* the known Earth Witches! Ellie couldn't quite believe it! She quickly grabbed the list of names and scanned it for the name, Dove — *Dove* it read!

Ellie quickly scrambled around looking for a piece of paper to write a reply. As she did, she looked over to the bird who was stretching its wings. It looked very tired. 'You poor thing,' Ellie spoke softly. 'You must be exhausted after your long flight.' 'Very,' the bird replied. Ellie was shocked to hear the bird speak so well. Remembering her manners, Ellie politely addressed the bird. 'You speak awfully well,' she said to it.

'What type of bird are you – if you don't mind me asking that is?'

The bird raised its beak proudly as it answered, 'I'm Amara the mynah bird, very pleased to meet you,' and with that she made a kind of bow. Ellie smiled and bowed back, 'Pleased to meet such a unique bird. Now you must be thirsty and hungry, let me get you something.' As Ellie went to fetch Amara some water and bread, she started to think about the request from Georgie Dove. She wondered how many Earth Witches would be at the gathering – how many would be from her list – and what sort of gathering it would be.

Amara was still perched on Ellie's desk when she returned to her room. Amara saw that Ellie was lost in thought. 'Why do you worry so?' she questioned Ellie. 'I'm not at all sure I should go to this meeting,' said Ellie, 'I don't know what I am getting myself into. Come to think about it, I don't even know where it's taking place.'

Amara hopped closer to Ellie 'You have to trust in yourself, Ellie – in your instincts. You are very powerful; I can sense it and I have seen it. The wild storms last year — we saw your power shine through. It is strong but you seem unsure of this.' Amara took a drink and then continued, 'Georgie is trying to revive the Earth Witchcraft, but cannot do it alone. The Earth Witches can help you understand your power and you can help to unite them all.' Ellie looked at Amara and then down at her acorn necklace which was still glowing. Learning more about the Earth Witchcraft excited Ellie. It was what she wanted to do. Her Weather Witch friends knew little of the Earth Witch magic and her mother had never truly practised the art. Ellie took a deep breath. 'Ok,' she said and with that she started to write a note for Amara to take to Georgie.

Ellie and Georgie wrote to each other often after that day, Ellie had many questions before the gathering was due to take place and her excitement grew with every letter.

It was three weeks ago that Amara had delivered the invitation to Ellie and now, finally, the day had come for her to go to meet Georgie and the other Earth Witches.

Ellie felt very nervous — she'd never been so far away from home on her own before. She wished Bryony could come with her, but Bryony had started her thunder and lightning training in the South so couldn't. Ellie still hoped she may be able to see Bryony there — if she had any breaks in her training that was.

Ellie put the last few bits in her backpack, adjusted her necklace then grabbed her broom and headed to the old oak tree at the bottom of her garden. There, waiting for her by the grand tree were four Weather Witches alongside her mother. The two oldest witches were her dear friends Elodie and Maeve Mayweather. They had become very frail since Ellie had first met them and their hair was now pure white — Elodie's hair almost looked like it was sparkling. Maeve gave Ellie a broad grin. Elodie however had a lost, faraway look on her face as she gave Ellie a small nod and slight smile. The other two Weather Witches were Bryony's mother and Hazel, Bryony's sister.

'Are you ready?' Hazel asked as she hugged Ellie. 'As ready as I'll ever be!' Ellie replied while mounting her broom. 'Don't worry you will have an amazing time,' Hazel reassured her. 'We're going to make mist for you to fly above,' she continued, showing off a little, 'it will help carry you along and shield you from curious eyes — it's such a long journey you can't do it all at night so best to start now. I've been practising and the mist will stay with you for pretty much the whole flight.' Then, lifting her weather stone to the sky, she spoke clearly 'Spéir ceobhránach tosnaigh!'* A thick mist started to appear and surround Ellie — lifting her broom slowly up.

---

* 'Spéir ceobhránach tosnaigh!' (spare keo-vrawn-uck tus-nig) — Irish/Gaeilge for foggy/misty skies

'Now Ellie, be safe, and let me know the minute you arrive!' Ellie's mother called up to her as she rose higher in the air. 'Good luck,' Maeve said and Elodie, still looking distant, turned to Ellie and said, 'Be safe Heather, make sure you don't lose your broom.'

Ellie looked confused. 'Elodie, I'm *Ellie* not my great grandmother Heather.' Elodie smiled and held Maeve's hand. 'Sorry,' she called, 'my head gets a little cloudy sometimes.' Then her face went very serious, and she looked straight up into Ellie's eyes. 'Beware of the síoga*. Beir greim ar do chrann scuaibe.'† 'Sorry,' Ellie stuttered, 'I don't understand.' But Elodie didn't repeat herself — instead, she just waved as Ellie flew higher.

Elodie's behaviour had worried Ellie but she knew she had to concentrate. She was going to be flying further than she had ever done before and needed to keep her wits about her.

---

*   Síoga (she-oh-ga) — Irish/Gaeilge for fairies
†   Beir greim ar do chrann scuaibe (bear grime air duh crown scuba) — Irish/Gaeilge for 'Hold onto your broom'

Chapter 2

The Song of the Fairies

Ellie had been flying for what seemed like ages when the mist began to fade and she could see mountains all around. Yes, she was sure she was in the right place — Georgie had described these mountains so well it was almost like she'd been here before — but where was Georgie?

Ellie landed and jumped off her broom. She looked around expecting to see her pen pal and the other Earth Witches but couldn't see anyone. Then, out of the corner of her eye, she thought she glimpsed a figure. Ellie rubbed her eyes and called out 'Georgie? Is that you?' The figure stopped abruptly, seeming startled, and started to walk slowly towards her.

'It's me, Ellie,' Ellie continued. As the figure got closer, Ellie could make out she was a girl and had blue curly hair. She was different to how Ellie had imagined her pen pal, but nevertheless she was pleased to see her.

'Yes, hi Ellie — sorry I was just lost in thought for a moment,' the girl said, her voice was soft and gentle, almost dream like. She looked at Ellie's broom and smiled 'You flew?' 'Yes,' Ellie answered 'I said I would be...'

'Yes, sorry, yes, of course you did,' replied her pen pal, 'where are my manners. Come, you should meet my family,' and with that she beckoned Ellie to follow her. Ellie picked up her broom and hurried after her pen pal who seemed to be almost floating down the mountainside. They hadn't been walking long when they arrived at the edge of a beautiful forest. Ellie didn't remember seeing the forest as she flew over but assumed the mist had still been too thick at that point and happily followed her friend in through the dense trees.

A sweet smell seemed to dance through the leaves of the magnificent trees, they were so tall they must have been there for hundreds of years. The forest though, seemed silent. Ellie couldn't hear any creatures or even her own footsteps. As she looked down at her feet, she heard a song echoing through the trees and the thoughts she had been having all suddenly disappeared. The song seemed to be calling her, she looked up and seeing her friend ahead realised the song was coming from her.

'Come follow me through the Forest of Dreams,
come follow me treading lightly.

Leaving no trace as we explore this place.
Come follow me, come follow me...'

Ellie was mesmerised, following her and her song deeper into the forest.

'Come see the trees reaching up to the sky,
feel their strong roots under earth where they lie —

Come follow me through the Forest of Dreams,
come follow me, come follow me...'

Ellie's legs began to feel heavy; her pen pal had also stopped walking and was now dancing around Ellie. Ellie could no longer lift her feet.

'Stand silently, though your heart will still beat,
feeling now roots where your feet used to be —

Come follow me through the Forest of Dreams,
come follow me, come follow me.'

Fear rose in Ellie's heart — something just didn't seem right. She glanced down. To her horror she saw her feet were no longer feet — roots had started sprouting from her shoes and were quickly burying themselves in the earth.

Ellie tried to scream but no sound came out, she closed her eyes. An image came to her mind, a crystal-clear image — it was of Elodie and Maeve in their study, chatting. Suddenly they stopped as if they could see Ellie watching them. Elodie turned and looked straight at her. 'Síoga!* Hold onto your broom!' called Elodie. Startled, Ellie opened her eyes and reached for her broom. A loud clatter of thunder rang out overhead. The song stopped. Ellie could move again. She glanced around, looking for the girl she'd been following, and as soon as her eyes found her, she saw her burst into hundreds of little creatures all screaming and frantically flying around — fairies!

Ellie desperately looked for her broom, as the tiny fairies flew all around her pulling at her hair, but it was nowhere to be seen. While batting the fairies away, Ellie looked up and, as she did, the trees around her faded and she saw she was still on the mountain top near to where she'd landed. The fairies fled.

---

*   Síoga (she-oh-ga) — Irish/Gaeilge for fairies

Ellie dropped to the ground. She screamed loudly, holding back tears of anger and frustration, then took a deep breath, closed her eyes, and listened. She heard the winds blowing through the peaks of the mountains, she heard birds singing in the far distance and heard the faint sound of moving water. Slowly she opened her eyes. Yes, she was in a new and strange land, but this was not the first time she'd been in a land strange to her. She was smart and strong; she knew she would need to retrace her footsteps and find her real pen pal Georgie. She knew she could do this.

Ellie stood up and put her backpack on. The views were spectacular, there were mountains for as far as her eyes could see. As Ellie looked around, she could see in the distance a group of five people waving to her, first walking, then running to get to her. At the front was a dark-haired boy with big brown eyes. He was smiling broadly, waving and every so often jumping into the air as he skipped over to Ellie. A mynah bird was flying close behind him. 'Ellie! Ellie! It's me, Georgie!'

'Georgie?' Ellie looked a little confused — she wasn't sure whether to believe him or not. She looked at the mynah bird who was now perched on his shoulder and smiled, relieved to see the familiar face. 'Hello again, Amara,' she said, then looking to the boy continued, 'Oh, Georgie, it *is* you, isn't it? Georgie, am I pleased to see you — something terrible has happened! I was so frightened....' but before she could tell him all that had happened....

'Where's your broom?' Georgie interrupted, 'I thought you said you'd be flying over?'

'That's what I'm trying to tell you, fairies tried to turn me into a tree and *stole* my broom!'

'Oh dear,' Georgie said looking down and fidgeting, 'I must have been late.'

'What do you mean, late?' Ellie quizzed.

'Ah, well that's the thing,' Georgie said, 'I should have been here yesterday it would seem, but I was here on a day that *felt* like a yesterday, but it actually turns out it was today... so I am here today, not yesterday.'

'I'm sorry?' Ellie was confused 'Yesterday? What day is today?'

'It must be Monday,' Georgie replied.

'Monday! I've been here a whole day already?! Are you sure? My mum will be so worried.' Georgie nodded and looked down. One of the others stepped forward. She was short and had her hair in a messy plait that fell halfway down her back. She reached out her hand to greet Ellie. 'Sorry Ellie,' said the girl, 'my cousin is fairly useless with days and time. My name is Ayda. Don't worry about your mum — we'll send word to her straight away, so she knows you're safe,' and with that the girl knelt down and placed both hands on the ground, as she did Ellie felt a small tremor go through the earth. 'There. The Earth will let your mum know you arrived here safely,' Ayda said while getting up from the ground and dusting off her knees.

Ellie shook her head as if to settle the jumble of thoughts that were flashing around in there, then took a proper look at the five people who had come to meet her. 'Is this everyone?' she asked, trying not to sound too disappointed, 'only five of you?'

'Six now,' Georgie said with a big smile. He then began to introduce Ellie to the others. 'You met my cousin Ayda, we live here in the mountains. This is Forest,' Georgie pointed to the very tall, fair-haired, boy stood behind him, 'he's travelled from further north than you.' Next to Forest stood a very slight girl, her hair fell in a neat bob, 'Rosie travelled from the East and this is Birdie – she's travelled from the West.' Birdie was tall and looked to be the eldest of the group. Ellie thought there was a motherly feel about her. Although there were only five of them, they had journeyed from all over the world to be there and each had a piece of jewellery with a different seed threaded onto it like Ellie's acorn necklace.

Rosie stepped forward. 'We are very pleased you are here, Ellie. Your power is very strong. We all saw it from our own countries. It was bright. It seemed new.' She spoke with a smile but could see Ellie was confused. 'You don't understand your power, do you?' Rosie said. Ellie shook her head, feeling almost ashamed. 'That's OK,' Rosie continued, 'we can help. We may be young, but we have learned to master our powers and can help you with yours.'

'I need my broom back,' Ellie said in a small voice. 'All in good time,' Birdie said. 'Let's eat and then we can plan. Come on let us go back to camp.'

Chapter 3

The Story in the Fire

Camp wasn't far and although it was small it looked comfortable. There were three small huts, one had vines, flowers, and butterflies all over it. 'That's where Forest is staying,' Ayda said to Ellie. 'He's only been here two days and already he's made friends with all the plants and creatures,' she chuckled. Forest smiled as he walked over to his hut and turned back to Ellie and Ayda with a shrug and remarked, 'What can I say? I'm a good listener,' and with that he went inside. He was so tall he had to bend a little to get into the door.

In the middle of the huts there was a small campfire. Georgie set about lighting it while Birdie fetched some food. The others sat down on the logs that were around the fire. It didn't take long for it to catch and burn brightly and for the dusk of the evening to set in. Ellie could hear the faint rumble of thunder in the distance.

The Earth Witches happily tucked into their food. Ellie ate more slowly than the others, still worrying about her broom and how she was going to get it back. Ayda, who was sat opposite Ellie, spoke to the group. 'We should go around, and each tell Ellie who we are and what magic we can do, kind of like a quick-fire, team-building experience.' She sounded very excited, and everyone agreed that this seemed like a fun idea. 'I'll go first,' she continued before anyone else had a chance. 'I'm Ayda. As Georgie said earlier, we live in these mountains and have done so our whole lives. I started practising the Earth Witchcraft when I was very young, and my skill is that I am able to move rocks!' She said this very proudly — Birdie and Forest sniggered. Ayda started to blush and slouched a little in her seat.

'Sorry Ayda,' Birdie chuckled, 'I can't help but think you must mean small little stones, you are so little yourself you couldn't possibly move much and I wouldn't call that a skill as such.'

'I may be small but I am mighty,' Ayda muttered to herself. Then finding her voice again she retorted, 'Well then what can you do — being the giants you are?'

Forest spoke confidently, 'I think all can see what I can do, I speak to the creatures and the plants.' Then with a smile he added, 'I'm a friendly giant.'

'And I, little one,' Birdie said, 'I can read and translate the many, ancient, magical scriptures of the lands.' Ayda crossed her arms grumpily and Birdie continued, 'Ayda, don't be like that – we joke. Relax.'

Ayda did not look up at Birdie but instead focused on the flames of the fire. Georgie, sensing the growing tension, took a seed from his pocket and threw it into the flames. It began to crackle and spark. Ellie looked over at Georgie and could see he was moving his hands in a very strange manner. She then glanced back to the flames which were now dancing high. As she looked, she could see they were changing shape and beginning to look like different things. Ellie was fascinated. The flames changed to people, to witches, Ellie could make out that all were wearing Earth Witch hats. They held hands and gathered in a circle. When the circle was complete, they changed into trees.

'I know this story,' Forest said, 'my family would tell me about the forest of the Ancient Elders and the magic grove they created to protect us all.' Georgie smiled, 'It's supposed to be a true story you know.' Ayda smiled too and leant into Georgie. 'It never fails to lift your mood Ayda,' he said with a grin.

Placing his hands down on his lap, the grove of trees became dancing flames once more.

'Wow,' Ellie said in amazement. 'Is that your power Georgie?'

Georgie replied, 'Kind of, I suppose, possibly, this would be more of a party trick. I can create and change energies — positive to negative that sort of thing. I found out I could use a different energy flow to manipulate the flames by accident really.'

'And the seed?' Ellie asked. 'The seed is a Phoenix Sequoia seed,' Georgie replied. 'The seed was to focus the flame's energy. Energy can be a tricky thing you know, so you must make sure there's a focus or a grounding element.'

Rosie nodded in agreement with Georgie, 'Yes, a grounding element is most important to have in all types of magic,' she said, then added, almost thinking aloud, 'magic has opposites; magic is powerful; never let it rule you; never try to rule it.' The group fell silent at these words. Rosie, seemingly embarrassed, suddenly stood up. 'Anyway, it's getting late, we should get some rest,' she said before rushing into her hut. 'That was odd,' Ayda remarked then followed Rosie's lead and headed to bed not too shortly after, followed by Forest and Birdie. Ellie and Georgie stayed by the fire.

'Why do you suppose Rosie left so abruptly Georgie?' Ellie asked in a whisper. Georgie shrugged as he put his hand in his pocket and retrieved another Phoenix Sequoia seed to toss into the fire. 'I'm not sure, it may have been to do with the story I was telling with the fire.' The seed he tossed into the fire began to spark and crackle, Ellie turned her attention once more to the flames.

'You see Ellie, ancient stories like this one change each time they are told. There are child friendly versions, most probably the one Forest so fondly remembers, but then there are also darker versions.' As Georgie spoke the flames came to life and once more Ellie could see the group of Earth Witch Ancient Elders gathering in the circle holding hands. Ellie focused hard on the flames and then began to feel a fluttering in her stomach — a mix of excitement and fear.

Suddenly she saw herself in the story, standing in the middle of the ancient elders' circle but she wasn't alone — a young Earth Witch also stood there. She seemed to be younger than Ellie and wore an Earth Witch hat with an unusual seed and leaf at the tip. Ellie could have sworn she recognised this seed but could not place where. The girl was obviously panicked as she looked from elder to elder with such fear in her eyes, sobbing, and shouting out, 'Please don't, not this, this power doesn't need to be feared I can master it, please give me time'.

Not only could Ellie feel the fear coming from this young girl, but she also felt the wall of hatred coming from the circle of elders surrounding them, closing in on them. Ellie and the girl crouched down covering their heads, what else could they do? Then Ellie realised she could hear Georgie's voice — she was not living this; she was still sitting with Georgie by the campfire.

'Stories are told of an Earth Witch,' Georgie was saying 'who, when only young, was cursed with Weather Witch powers.' 'Why do you say cursed?' Ellie quizzed, offended by Georgie's remark. He quickly continued, 'That's just the way the story has been told. You see, they believed she was cursed as she could never control the powers of the weather however hard she tried. Storms would follow her when she was sad, blistering sun when she was happy, there was never a middle ground. The elders were frightened — not only for her but for everyone around her. They became angry in their fear and finally gathered together and with force changed her into a tree in order to ground her powers and save her.'

The flames, still holding the image of the ancient elders' circle started to rise in the middle — higher and higher — as the young girl, trapped, started to take the form of a tree. The fire crackled with intensity, Ellie saw the tree suddenly crack and split almost in two. Then one by one the elders became trees also. As Ellie watched, Georgie continued.

'You see, legend says that because the ancient elders could not manage to stop the weather from targeting her, they too were compelled to change to trees to try to contain the damage being caused. No one is a hundred per cent sure how much of the story is true, but there is definitely a Forest of the Ancient Elders – though I have never been – and there are people who swear there is a magic grove there which no one can enter.'

Georgie began to yawn and the flames became ordinary flames once more, slowly dying as they settled to embers. 'Rosie may not have liked the story,' Georgie said, 'she may have been familiar with a scarier version.'

Something about the story didn't sit right with Ellie. She couldn't believe that Rosie had just been too scared of it to want to stay up. The seed on the Earth Witch's hat, too, kept replaying in her mind as she tried to figure out where she'd seen it before. 'Hmm maybe, but I'm not too sure,' Ellie said as she headed to the hut she was sharing with Birdie. Neither Ellie nor Georgie had noticed Rosie peeping out from her hut as she listened silently.

Chris

Chapter 4

Into the Fairy Woods

The next day the sun shone, and the group awoke refreshed and ready for an adventure. Rosie was the first up and was busily writing in her notebook while the others started to rise and get ready for the day.

After breakfast all six of them gathered in the centre of the huts making sure they all were prepared for the day ahead. 'Where's Amara?' Ellie asked, noticing she was missing. 'Here and there, not sure, she just comes and goes really. But don't worry I'm sure we'll see her again at some point,' Georgie replied, putting the last few bits in his backpack. 'Of course,' Ellie thought to herself, 'Amara is a free wild bird not a pet'.

Ellie was nervous about going to the fairy woods but also still angry at them for stealing her broom. Georgie could see this in her face, 'Fairies aren't really bad,' Georgie explained, 'you would have only been a tree for a day or so. They must have thought you were a Weather Witch. Fairies and Weather

Witches do not get on well at all, that was probably why they stole your broom.'

'Well, that doesn't sound like something a nice person would do,' Ellie grumpily replied. 'I need to get my broom back.'

'And we will, don't worry. We'll just have to find the Fairy Queen and ask her,' Georgie said matter- of-factly.

'Just *ask* her?' Ellie quizzed.

'Well, she may want something in return, but we'll see. Now which way should we go Ellie?'

Ellie was shocked that Georgie was asking *her* which way, how was she supposed to know? Georgie could see by the look on her face she had no idea what he meant.

'Listen, just listen,' Georgie said almost in a whisper. 'You will know where to go.'

Ellie closed her eyes and listened, willing herself to hear something, though unsure what. As she did, she heard the birds singing in the distance and wind blowing gently through the leaves of trees. Still with her eyes closed, she turned to the left and there was silence, she could not hear any sounds coming from this new direction. She raised her hand and pointed. She opened her eyes and said confidently, 'This way, this is where I am being told to go.'

With a broad grin Georgie jumped up. 'What are we waiting for then? Come on everyone!' With that everyone grabbed their belongings and off they went, Ellie and Georgie in front and the others close behind.

It wasn't long before they came to a wooded area. Ellie felt a little unsure as one by one they stepped into the wood.

Rosie turned to her, 'Don't be afraid, here take this, it's my lucky stone and has always brought me courage, perhaps it will do the same for you,' and with that Rosie handed Ellie a grey stone with one smooth end and the other jagged as if it were missing a piece. As Ellie took the stone, she noticed the seed on Rosie's ring.

'That's where I've seen that seed before!' Ellie suddenly exclaimed. 'That's the same seed as the Earth Witch's in the story Georgie told us yesterday!'

Rosie blushed and pulled her hand quickly away. 'Georgie must have noticed it earlier in the day and got the story muddled slightly, that's all,' Rosie stuttered and walked off into the forest. Ellie didn't know how, but felt she had offended Rosie. Rosie walked too quickly away for her to apologise so Ellie looked ahead at the forest. She held onto the lucky stone, and she listened — she could hear the sounds of the woodland life around her and instantly felt calmer as she followed the others in through the trees.

A little way into the wood, they came to a tree that had fallen over the path. The tree was not too much of a bother — they had the choice of going up and over the trunk or through the thinner branches that would have been at the top of the tree. Georgie looked at Ellie. It was clear she was going to go through the branches so Georgie, walking next to her, followed. The rest of the group climbed up and over the trunk.

When Ayda, Forest, Rosie and Birdie reached the top of the trunk and looked down to where Ellie and Georgie should have been coming out from the branches, there was no sign of them. It was like they had vanished into thin air.

'Right. Set up camp here,' Birdie instructed taking charge of the remaining group, 'they may be a while.'

'Why didn't we all go in?' Forest asked as he examined the fallen tree.

Rosie answered him. 'That way leads to the Fairy Woods,' she said, 'only two people would ever be allowed to enter at any one time. The Fairy Queen would never risk allowing more than that. Three is a very powerful number in magical realms you know.' Rosie spoke with authority. Forest nodded in response and the four of them started to set up a small shelter to await their friends' return.

Now, although the branches had looked quite thin when Ellie and Georgie had started, it turned out that this was not the case at all. The branches were actually thick and full of leaves. As the friends walked, the leaves seemed to become thicker and Ellie smelt a familiar sweet smell in the air. When they finally emerged from the tree, they both realised they were no longer in the same woods and they were no longer with the other Earth Witches.

This wood was very different to 'normal' woods — the trees and plants were muted pastel shades and all were glistening like the frost on a crisp winter morning. The air smelled sweet and the breeze was warm and pleasant.

'You did it!' Georgie said excitedly with a little hop and a skip.

Slowly smiling Ellie said, 'I did, didn't I? Now what?' She looked at Georgie, he shrugged his shoulders. 'Not sure, I suppose they will come to us. It's not every day people enter the Fairy Woods.'

'Will they be angry?' Ellie asked, her voice wavering a little. 'Nah... Maybe... We'll soon see,' Georgie said pointing straight ahead.

Hundreds of fallen petals were dancing in the breeze and heading towards them. The closer they got Ellie realised that they were not petals at all but fairies — hundreds of small, delicate fairies, each dressed in a different coloured petal.

There was a loud chattering coming from the flurry of fairies, they all seemed to be talking at once.

'What are they doing here?' one asked.

'Isn't that your one from the mountain top?' another replied.

'Who's that with her?' said one as she flew past Georgie's head. 'He looks like an Earth Witch,' she continued, her head to one side as she squinted at him.

'Yeah he looks harmless,' the others agreed, 'she looks suspicious though — don't trust her.'

'We must send for the Queen, she'll be furious they've entered our woods,' one fairy in a yellow petal said and they all shuddered with fear for a second.

'We should — you go,' another said to the fairy in yellow.

'Why me?' he protested.

'She likes you,' was the response.

'But, but, but. Urgh. Ok I'll go.' The fairy sighed, shoulders drooped and flew off into the woods.

The other fairies all looked at one another. 'What should we do while we wait for the Queen?' one asked.

'We need to keep them here,' said another.

'Yes, we need to make sure they don't get any further into the woods,' another agreed.

'How do we do that?' asked the first fairy.

'Should we attack?' suggested a further fairy.

'Not sure — should we?' They muttered to each other, then all agreeing, one spoke, 'Right so — ATTACK!'

All the fairies then launched themselves at Ellie and Georgie, pulling at their hair and biting them.

The friends batted the fairies away as best they could but there was so many of them. Georgie started to mutter some words under his breath and his bracelet began to glow. The ground began to vibrate and trees around them began to shake. The fairies noticed and started to retreat. 'How are you doing that?' Ellie whispered to Georgie, he looked towards her and replied, 'I'm not doing anything, I hadn't finished the spell yet.' The vibrations stopped and Ellie gulped as she looked around, scared of what had caused the shaking. Georgie's bracelet stopped glowing.

Suddenly the breeze picked up and a flurry of leaves and dirt swirled up from the ground. A light glistened so brightly Ellie and Georgie had to shield their eyes for a moment. As the leaves and dirt settled and their eyes adjusted to the light, they saw a glistening, majestic, figure standing before them. This fairy stood taller than the rest, a crown of delicate flowers rested on her golden hair. There was no mistaking it — this was the Fairy Queen.

The Fairy Queen looked at Ellie and spoke sternly, 'You have entered our woods without an invitation or a guide — what makes you think you are welcome?'

Ellie was scared, she wasn't really sure how to respond. She cleared her throat and tried to stop her voice from shaking, 'Your fairies took something special from me and I would like it back... please.'

The fairies began to chatter loudly. The Fairy Queen raised her hand and there was silence. 'Oh, so you are the child I have heard whispers about.' The Fairy Queen stepped towards the friends as she spoke, never taking her eyes off Ellie. 'A child that arrives from the sky wearing an Earth Witch's necklace yet riding on a Weather Witch's broom?' She stared hard at them as she questioned. Ellie felt a shiver up her spine. 'Perhaps *you* took these from others?' the Fairy Queen said more sharply and directly to Ellie, ignoring Georgie completely.

'Please,' Ellie stuttered, 'the necklace is my Great Grandmother's, and the broom was given to me as a thank you gift. I would never take anything that wasn't mine and I need to have the broom back to get home.' The Fairy Queen thought and then said, 'So, you expect me to give you 'back' something my fairies *found* but offer nothing in return for my kind gesture?'

Ellie chortled and blurted out almost by accident, 'Found it — they stole it!'

'Silence!' the Fairy Queen demanded. Ellie, surprised at the strength of the Fairy Queen's retort, stepped back, eyes wide with fear. The fairies instantly stopped their chattering and became very still. They could feel the Queen's disapproval of their actions and like naughty children, they felt ashamed. Slowly, her piercing eyes still fixed unblinking on Ellie, the Fairy Queen spoke, 'There are three things I need that my fairies cannot get for me. Three things that only Earth Witches can deliver. The only way you will get your broom back is if you bring to me what I demand!'

The Fairy Queen leant forward, 'Now be gone and do not return to MY woods until your task is complete.' As she spoke a large leaf floated down from the trees above and landed in Ellie's hand. Ellie looked at the leaf and saw it had some sort of beautiful, delicate writing on it.

Ellie looked blankly at the letters. Beautiful though they were they made no sense to her. 'But I can't read this. How will I know what to get?' Ellie quizzed — but as she looked up there were no fairies to be seen — only Georgie next to her looking just as bewildered as she felt.

'Where did they go?'

Georgie spoke quietly, 'Dunno, they just disappeared.'

Suddenly their surroundings changed, and they were back at the woods with the other four witches, who looked equally as shocked to see them. 'Y- y- you just appeared,' stuttered Forest, 'out of thin air.'

'And you were only gone a couple of seconds,' Ayda said shocked, adding, 'did you even get to meet the Fairy Queen?' Ellie and Georgie nodded, still trying to figure out how they were back with the others. 'Yes,' Ellie said slowly, 'yes, we met her, she didn't like me. She's demanded these things.' Ellie started to explain to the others showing them the leaf. 'But I have no idea what this all means on here.'

Birdie took the leaf from Ellie and studied the lettering on it closely. 'This is ancient fairy script,' she said as her eyes followed the loops and curls of the words, 'I haven't seen this exact type or dialect before.'

'Can you read it?' Ayda asked. 'Of course I can,' Birdie said confidently, 'just give me a while to fully focus.' Still holding the leaf, Birdie sat on the trunk of the fallen tree and started to hum a strange tune.

Chapter 5

A Flower of Blue

After just a few moments Birdie jumped to her feet and walked over to Ellie. 'Here,' she said pointing to the first line, 'this word here means flower, the one next to it is blue — the Fairy Queen wants a flower of blue, a blue flower.' Birdie had a big grin on her face.

'That's amazing how you can understand what it says — thank you,' Ellie said.

'The rest I will need more time with, but we can start there,' Birdie said, pre-empting the group's next questions.

'I've heard the insects talk of a blue flower — I could ask where they would grow?' offered Forest. As he spoke a beautiful butterfly fluttered by and landed on his shoulder. Forest smiled, 'Glow will guide us there.' With that the group happily set off following Glow, the butterfly, out of the forest. What a peculiar thing, Ellie thought with a smile, as she walked.

The sun shone brightly overhead and the group cheerily continued on their trek. Ellie looked on in amazement as Forest seemed to be in deep conversation with their butterfly guide.

'How does he do that?' Ellie whispered to Ayda.

'It's his power, so no one apart from him really knows,' she replied. 'Apparently he's been chatting to creatures and plants since he was a toddler. I tried once, but I don't have the patience. He is a bit of a chatterbox though,' Ayda added, rolling her eyes.

The six friends followed Glow to a mountain and were very excited when they saw blue flowers of all shapes and sizes before them. Ellie, Georgie, Ayda, Birdie and Rosie all jumped with joy and ran over to the sea of blue plants. Forest, however, stayed back and shook his head.

'Friends,' he said solemnly, 'this isn't right, these aren't really blue. Look — they are all different types of flowers.' As he spoke, the group looked closer. Glow fluttered around them and as she landed on each flower the blue colour changed. Some turned to pink, some to red, until there were no more blue flowers left.

'Fairy tricks,' Rosie muttered. Ellie, who was stood beside her, heard and sighed. The breeze began to blow a little colder. Rosie noticed the change. Taking out her notebook she quickly scribbled something down and then put it back. Glow indicated to Forest that they had to continue up the mountainside and so the friends began to climb higher.

The higher they got, the more Ellie couldn't believe that a flower, let alone such a delicate one, would be able to grow here, but as soon as that thought entered her head, she noticed a blue smudge on the ground just ahead. As they moved closer the group could see quite clearly it was a blue poppy and knew that this must be the blue flower the Fairy Queen had asked for. Ellie ran over to it — excited that they had found the first of the three items needed for her to get her broom back. She leant down and looked at this beautiful flower, so unique in colour, in fact quite unique all together. She looked around and realised that it was the only one on the whole mountainside where they stood. Ellie wandered around, thinking. Forest meanwhile said his 'Thank yous' to Glow who was still resting on his shoulder and the butterfly fluttered its wings and flew over to the poppy, landing gently on the petals.

'What's wrong?' Georgie asked Ellie. 'What are you thinking?'

'This is a rare flower,' Ellie stated, 'very rare. I can't see any more anywhere here.' Georgie began to look around too and realised his friend was right; he began to get a sinking feeling. Ellie looked at him and he knew she was feeling the same.

'I don't feel I can pick this flower,' she said, 'it's so rare, so beautiful, it doesn't feel right.' 'But what about the Fairy Queen and your broom?' Ayda quizzed, as she walked up to Ellie and Georgie, but Ellie just shrugged in response and put her backpack back on. A cold breeze blew through the mountains.

The rest of the group picked up their backpacks too. Georgie smiled, 'Onwards and upwards,' he declared and with a hop and a skip he walked past the poppy and headed up the mountainside.

'Where to next?' Ayda asked Birdie who had been studying the Fairy Queen's instructions. 'This is a tricky part,' Birdie began. 'This first bit looks like the word for Dragon but the flick on the final symbol could make it mean something different entirely.'

Rosie looked to where Birdie was pointing then turned to Georgie and Ayda. 'Am I right in thinking there is a cave known as the Dragon's cave near here?' Georgie did a little jump 'Yes,

yes, you're absolutely right!' he replied excitedly, turning to his left, 'Let's aim for the Dragon's cave — this way!' Ayda shook her head. 'This way,' she said holding Georgie's shoulders and turning him to the right. Georgie, undeterred, smiled and hopped and skipped to his right, 'This way!' he said.

Chapter 6

The Dragon's Cave

As they continued to walk, Ellie looked down at the rocky ground. To her surprise she saw lots of red and orange oak leaves, 'Autumn?' she muttered to herself, confused as to why there were oak leaves, as she had not seen an oak tree since she had left her garden.

She raised her voice slightly, 'Autumn already? How long have we been here?' she looked desperately at Georgie. He turned to her confidently and said, 'Don't worry, what you see is not what you see.' Rosie added, 'The fairies are playing tricks on you, reminding you of home and trying to trick you into thinking you've been here months. We must be close to where we need to be and they're trying to stop us.'

Ellie felt reassured. 'But how come they are not affecting any of you?' she asked looking at the group. As she looked around at the others, she noticed each of the seeds they wore was glowing. 'We have protection against the fairy's tricks, you see

— my seed ring is glowing,' Rosie said to Ellie, 'it is using its power to protect me — you can do this too.'

'Hold your necklace in your left hand,' Birdie instructed Ellie. 'Picture a bubble that surrounds you — your acorn should begin to glow and then you're protected.' Ellie did as Birdie had said and sure enough her necklace began to glow. As she continued to walk Ellie couldn't help but keep looking at the glowing acorn, turning it over in her hand. She was so proud she had been able to do this spell.

Suddenly someone grabbed her arm, 'Stop! You nearly walked over the edge!' Ayda shouted.

The group of friends found themselves standing at the edge of a steep cliff. Many miles below, water flowed into a cave that seemed to lead inside the cliff where they stood. 'This must be the dragon's cave,' Georgie said. 'We have to jump.'

'Jump?!' Ellie repeated, shocked and scared by the idea. 'But that's such a deep drop, we'd never survive.' Why wasn't anyone else horrified by the idea of jumping off a cliff, Ellie asked herself, seeing the others seemingly OK with the idea.

'Sure we will,' said Georgie, 'how else would we be able to get into the cave?' Ellie frantically looked for a safer way down and wished she had her broom back.

As she searched, Georgie put down his rucksack and began to pull out some ropes and carabiners. Ellie sighed with relief. 'Abseiling down you mean!'

'Of course that's what I mean,' Georgie said, laughing. 'You didn't think I meant jump off a steep cliff with no rope did you? That'd be way too dangerous!' and continuing to set up his abseiling equipment, he began to mutter and chuckle to himself. 'Jump off a cliff? With no rope? How silly, I haven't got nearly enough spare wingsuits for that.' The others also chuckled, and Ellie couldn't help but blush a little with embarrassment. Ayda put her hand on Ellie's shoulder, 'Don't worry Ellie, Georgie never really thinks sentences through before he speaks.'

Georgie was the last to reach the ground and as he did, he saw the others all staring at a pile of large boulders that were blocking the entrance.

'How are we going to get in?' Forest asked.

'Could we move the boulders by hand?' Ellie said thinking out loud. 'No — I doubt we'd be able to move one even if all of us were pushing together,' Birdie replied. Georgie smiled and did his hop and skip over to Ayda. He placed his arm over her shoulder and announced to the group, 'Ayda has this, right Ayda?'

Ayda turned bright red as the group turned and looked at her. Birdie, without realising, raised an eyebrow in disbelief. How was such a slight girl going to be able to move boulders as big as houses? Shrugging Georgie's arm off her shoulder, Ayda could see they all thought the same and she had never felt so small.

Ellie stepped towards Ayda, 'Do you really have the power to move rock? Georgie has told me all about your Great Grandmother, she was famous for moving mountains right?' Ellie said. Ayda looked up at Ellie and smiled. 'And didn't she also wear a Moringa seed?' Ellie continued, 'I'd love to see your power.'

Ayda pulled her shoulders back and stood as tall as she could, then, moving towards the group she said, 'I'd step back if I were you.'

Walking towards the blocked entrance of the cave Ayda raised her hands up towards the boulders and her necklace began to glow. She glanced back at the group, 'Maybe take shelter too — rocks sometimes explode when I do this.' With that Ayda turned back to face the boulders, her hands raised in front of her, her necklace glowing a bright yellow.

Ellie peered out from where she was sheltering, watching as the small stones all around Ayda began to rise up in the air. Ayda's plait also seemed to be rising up as the boulders began to tremble. The trembling turned into a violent shaking, cracks appeared down the great rocks as they began to glow. Ellie ducked back down just as the boulders exploded.

Birdie suddenly leapt out from her hiding spot and darted towards Ayda. 'Ayda, are you ok?' she shouted.

Ayda was now crouched on the floor. Slowly she stood up and dusted herself off. She turned and smiled, 'I did it!'

Birdie swept Ayda up in a strong embrace. 'Wow! Well done mighty Ayda!' she said as she swung her around. Slowly the rest of the group came out of their hiding places and walked towards the cave entrance.

The cave was large and dark. Ayda placed her hand on the cave wall, 'Let's have some light shall we?' and as she spoke the veins of quartz that ran through the rock began to glow, lighting the friends' way.

Ellie repeated the Fairy Queen's instructions. 'So, we think it says "capture a dragon of green". How do you capture a dragon? Dragons don't exist.'

'Not any more but the legend says that a tribe called the Dragonfeet used to be the protectors of dragons,' Rosie said and Georgie nodded in agreement. 'My favourite stories are of the Dragonfeet Tribe,' he added with a smile.

'Dragonfeet... Dragonfoot! The legend of Dragonfoot! I have that book! Hazel told me to read it.' Ellie excitedly got out the red tattered book. Georgie's face dropped; his smile was gone 'How did you get that book?'

'I *told* you my friend Hazel the Weather Witch gave it to me the night we defeated the wild storms.' She looked around at all the dismayed faces.

'That book was entrusted with the Earth Witches but many years ago it went missing — believed to be stolen,' Birdie told Ellie looking at her oddly.

'Hazel would have never stolen it,' Ellie said, remembering the night of the storms and remembering Audra the Weather Witch saying with such anger in her that *she* had helped defeat the Earth Witches — could this have been Audra's doing? Could she have stolen this book? Ellie dismissed the thought for a moment and brought her mind back to the task at hand.

'I'm sorry,' she said. 'I do not know how she had it, but it is with me now and it can help us here, please, please believe me.'

Georgie's smile slowly started to return, 'Of course I will, this is our adventure, and it's true the book will help. It's almost legend in our community may I see?' He stepped towards Ellie eager to look at the book but afraid to touch it — worried he may tear it or something — nervously, the others all stepped closer too.

'That symbol,' Georgie pointed to an image in the book though careful not to touch it, 'I think that's what we need to look for.'

The picture was a mixture of circles, lines and dots depicting a primitive image of a winged creature. 'Do you think it is a carving or a cave drawing perhaps?' Ellie asked. Georgie shrugged, 'It looks like it could be and we're in a cave, so I think it's worth looking for.' The friends, book in hand, started to look at all the walls in the cave, searching for the symbol of the winged creature.

'I hear chattering in the walls,' Forest said as he looked around, 'It gets louder over here.' He walked deeper into the cave. When he reached what he thought was the back of the cave he noticed the cave split into two different pathways. Forest stood silently listening carefully, first down one pathway and then down the next. 'Definitely down this one,' he muttered to himself as he started down the narrower of the two paths, bending down as he went further in.

Meanwhile the others were still looking high and low in the main part of the cave. They'd found a few spiders and interesting looking stones, but no symbols drawn on or carved into the rock. Ellie was starting to lose hope. Rosie held her hand, 'Don't worry we'll find it Ellie,' she said. 'But this cave is so large what if we lose our way?' Ellie replied. 'Don't worry,' Birdie said, 'As long as we all stick together we'll be fine.' As the last words left her lips, Ayda chirped, 'Where's Forest?' Birdie rolled her eyes. The group started to call for Forest. 'He couldn't have gone far,' Birdie said, 'it's not *that* big a cave.' 'I wouldn't be too sure about that,' Ayda said as she pointed to the two different pathways at the back of the cave. 'Oh, good grief,' Birdie groaned, 'How are we supposed to figure out which one he went down?' Georgie went to say 'We should split up' but Birdie, sensing his suggestion, stopped him before he could even open his mouth. 'No!' she said sharply, 'We don't know how long and winding these paths are — we could all get completely lost — we must stick together.' Ayda stepped forward and speaking gently suggested, 'I could try to see if I could feel the vibrations of Forest's steps through the rocks?' Ellie added, 'And if we stay really quiet, we could maybe listen down each path and see if we can hear him at all?' Birdie nodded. 'Excellent ideas,' she said.

Ayda knelt down and placed her hand on the cold rock floor in front of the first passage; the others, in silence, listened intently. Ayda's moringa seed on her necklace began to glow, her eyes closed. Slowly the glowing dulled and she shook her head. 'I can only feel stillness down that passage. Let's look at the next one — he must be down that one.' Again, Ayda took her knelt position and the others listened in silence. The necklace began to glow and pulse slightly this time. Ayda grinned wide and nodded, 'Yes, he's definitely down here,' she said confidently. They started heading down the second path. 'One second,' Ayda said as she placed her hand on the wall of the cave, 'let's have some light so we can see better.' As she spoke, the quartz in the rock started to glow again, making enough light to see down the narrow winding path. Suddenly they heard Forest's voice — 'Guys, you're here — look, come and look — I think I've found it!' He spoke excitedly as he emerged from around a bend in the path, unaware of the panic his disappearance had caused.

'Here!' he continued saying to the group as he turned and headed back down from where he'd just appeared. 'I've found it! It's here!' Birdie wanted to tell him off but was just too pleased to see him and excited to see the symbol.

Forest reached up to where the symbol had been carved into the wall of the cave, tracing over the lines with his fingers. 'The chattering is really loud here; can you guys hear it?' he asked as the others reached him. They all stood in silence and listened.

'Yes, I hear *something*,' the others began to say, each stepping closer to the wall listening as hard as they could. Suddenly, Forest's hand pressed against the carving and the stone moved slightly. He stepped back startled. Everyone stood still as they heard what had started as a small chattering begin to get louder and louder, and closer and closer. The sound was of fluttering wings, hundreds and hundreds of wings all manically flying. Suddenly, a huge mass of dragonflies flew out of the hole, over the group of friends, aiming for the cave's entrance.

'Green dragonflies!' Birdie shouted. 'It read *dragonflies*!' The group watched as the dragonflies flew out of the cave and into the dusky skies. One dragonfly, though, stayed by the entrance of the cave happily resting on part of a broken boulder. Ellie watched in wonder as it spread out its translucent wings. Night had begun to fall, and Ellie was having a dilemma about whether or not she could or would trap the dragonfly in a jar for the Fairy Queen.

'It just doesn't seem right to me,' she said to her friend, Georgie. 'Me neither,' he replied. 'We'll stay here tonight, and we can decide what to do next in the morning. The thunderstorms are on their way I can hear the rumble in the distance.'

'Does it thunder every night here?' Ellie asked.

'During this season yes – I think that's why the fairies have such an issue with the Weather Witches – it's dangerous for them to fly when there is so much thunder and lightning in the air.' Ellie could understand Georgie's point and pulled her shrug around her tightly as she watched the skies outside the cave light up. She couldn't help but smile though as she thought of her friend Bryony helping the thunder to roll and the lightning to clash. Before she knew it, she'd drifted off into a deep sleep.

Chapter 7

Fallen Leaves

The sun shone so brightly the next day it lit up the front of the cave and the quartz within the grey stone walls sparkled. Ellie had slept peacefully that night knowing she had done the right thing by not plucking the blue flower and not capturing the green dragonfly. Rosie was up and jotting down notes in her book like always. She looked up and smiled at Ellie. 'You seem in a good mood,' she said. 'Yes, I am,' Ellie replied with a smile. 'I think today will be a good day.' Rosie looked up to the sky. 'Hmmm and the sun is shining,' she muttered and began to write in her notebook again. Birdie was also up and stretched her arms wide, 'It always shines here, doesn't it?'

'Normally I'd agree,' Georgie said as he emerged from the cave, 'but the weather has been a little odd the past few days.' Before he could say anything else, Ayda came skipping out asking, 'Where to next Birdie?'

Birdie took a big sip of her drink and rubbed her eyes still trying to fully wake up. She took out the Fairy Queen's leaf and looked at it. 'The last line,' she began slowly, half yawning, 'says about a golden leaf. It's not clear if it is made out of gold or just a golden colour.'

Ayda jumped up and down excitedly. 'Oh, we know where this is Georgie,' she said. 'Our grandparents used to take us there when we were little.' Georgie remembered too and knew it wasn't very far from where they were. 'If we leave soon,' he said, 'we'll be there before noon.'

Everyone packed their bags and got ready for the final task ahead. As they walked away from the Dragon's Cave, Ellie looked back and smiled. She couldn't put her finger on why, but she felt calm and happy by the cave. She knew she would remember this journey forever.

The sun shone brightly and although the friends walked at a slower pace in the heat it wasn't long before they came to a beautiful tree standing solitary ahead of them.

The tree stood proud, and the golden leaves sparkled in the midday sun. Its beauty almost took the six friends' breath away.

'So, we climb the tree and pick a leaf?' Georgie asked looking at Ellie and examining the tree from where they stood. 'Yes, I suppose at least that way I would have one thing the Fairy Queen requested,' Ellie replied. She continued in jest, 'She may give me a *bit* of my broom back.' 'Yeah, maybe a splinter,' Georgie joked. The friends chuckled as they walked up to the golden-leafed tree.

Georgie and Ellie began to climb the tree as the others stood by the bottom. As they started to find their footholds on the trunk, Ellie glanced down and noticed there were two leaves lying on the ground and although they were still the unusual shape of the golden leaves on the tree, they were no longer golden at all but silver.

'Wait!' Ellie shouted.

Georgie stopped climbing and looked down at Ellie who had jumped from the tree and picked up one of the fallen leaves. 'Look,' she said waving the silver leaf at him, 'once picked they are no longer golden.'

The rest of the group gathered around Ellie and looked at the leaves — firstly the silver one in Ellie's hand and then the golden ones that moved in the breeze — happily clinging to the branches of this unique tree. Ellie sighed a big sigh and dropped her head, resting it against the tree's trunk. Silence. Then a very faint sound. Breathing. Ellie looked to Forest and said with a whisper, 'Can you hear that?' Forest placed his ear against the trunk. As they listened, he too could hear the tree breathing, almost singing as it did.

'I won't pick one,' Ellie said defiantly.

'Thank you,' a rustling whisper came from deep within the tree. Ellie placed her hand and forehead back on the trunk in response, then turned and began to walk away.

'Wait for me!' Georgie called as he leapt down from the tree and did a walk and a skip to catch up with his friend.

'Wait, Ellie,' Rosie said softly, 'may I have the leaves?'

Ellie gave Rosie the silver leaves she'd picked up from the ground. Rosie took them carefully and placed them on a low branch of the tree. She folded her hands around the leaves and the branch and her ring began to glow. She closed her eyes briefly then released her hands to reveal the two leaves now glistening golden as they clung once again to the tree.

Rosie smiled and then turned to catch up with the group. Ellie beamed at Rosie's kind gesture but couldn't help feeling a little bit upset at not having been able to get *any* of the items requested by the Fairy Queen.

She walked on, slightly ahead of the group, her footsteps heavier than before and she noticed a cooler breeze had started to blow. Rosie began to jot something down in her notebook once more.

'Why do you keep writing things down in that?' Birdie asked, 'What are you writing anyway?' She peered over Rosie's shoulder. Rosie seemed shocked and quickly shut the book. 'Err nothing, I just like to take notes that's all.' She stuffed the notebook safely back in her bag then hurriedly walked on ahead of Birdie.

Birdie turned to Ayda speaking quietly, 'Rosie's always taking notes. Do you ever wonder what she's writing down? Do you think she's writing things about us?' Ayda shrugged dismissively in response to Birdie's questions, but it did make her even more curious about the book, as she too had noticed Rosie acting strangely lately.

Chapter 8

The Mark of the Lightning

The breeze began lightly, but swiftly grew stronger and colder. The air was becoming thicker and dark clouds were accumulating behind the group. Georgie had noticed that this strange weather pattern seemed to be following them — in the distance the skies were blue. Was this another fairy trick, he wondered, but quickly dismissed that thought. Fairies wouldn't make a storm — that was not their style. He looked to the others, all of whom had begun to wrap themselves up a little more. Georgie then looked ahead at Ellie and saw there was a light glow around her. Could it be that Ellie, an *Earth* Witch, was conjuring up a storm? He did his hop and a skip to catch up to her.

'Ellie,' he said. Ellie didn't respond. Georgie saw her acorn necklace was glowing. 'Ellie,' he said again, louder. She glanced up and he saw tears in her eyes. 'Ellie, you have to stop and talk to me,' he grabbed her arm and she stopped.

'I know you're frustrated but do you see what you are doing?' he gestured up to the sky at the storm cloud that was now over their heads.

'How could I have done that?' Ellie snapped. 'Storms happen all the time, I'm not a Weather Witch — I don't even know if I am cut out to be an Earth Witch,' she shrugged his arm away.

Ayda, who had heard this exchange and seen Ellie's acorn necklace glow too, stepped forward 'What exactly happened when you were in the land behind the clouds with the Weather Witches. Did you touch something you shouldn't have — maybe the weather rock or something? If you did, it may be that some Weather Witch power transferred to you.'

Ellie looked down and remembered the night of the wild storms — how she'd stumbled and steadied herself on the Weather Rock. 'Can that happen?' Ellie asked quietly. 'Yes, it can,' Birdie replied joining them. With that Ellie burst out crying, 'I didn't know — how can I stop it? I should never have come here!' The storm above rumbled as Ellie spoke.

Georgie put his hands on Ellie's cheeks and stared into her eyes. 'Just breathe,' he said. 'I can help but you must help yourself too. Now, take deep breaths,' he instructed, firmly but kindly. Ellie took a deep breath in and as she breathed out, she saw Georgie's bracelet beginning to glow.

Georgie never broke eye contact and kept his hands gently on her face as she continued to take deep breaths. As she breathed in and out Ellie began to feel lighter and the storm clouds began to fade, her tears stopped, she closed her eyes. As she did, she felt Georgie's hands slip from her face. She opened her eyes to see Georgie collapsed onto the ground, his bracelet, no longer glowing, was now grey.

Ayda ran over to him and held his head in her lap, 'Georgie, you used too much energy,' she said, her voice shaking.

'It worked though,' Georgie replied, his voice very frail.

'You need to help him,' Ayda said looking up at Ellie.

'How?' Ellie replied.

'You have a bit of all our powers — you must try — maybe you can give back some of the energy?' Ayda replied with an urgency bordering on panic.

Ellie knelt down beside Georgie and placed her hands on his face as he had done to her and tried to channel her positive energy in order to send some to him. At first it appeared to work, his bracelet began to glow faintly, but it was clear Ellie didn't have enough power to save Georgie. He began to close his eyes. Ellie's thoughts raced, she had to think of a plan and fast. Energy was needed. Suddenly Ellie knew what she had to do. She stood up, stared up to the skies and focused. Within seconds a girl was zooming through the air and aiming straight towards them.....

'I'm here to save the day again!' Bryony announced as she landed in front of the group.

At first Ellie was taken aback by Bryony's comment and then, 'Ohhh! You did the lightning clash stopping the fairies! I thought maybe....! Thank you!' Ellie excitedly hugged Bryony, then, remembering the task at hand pointed to Georgie.

'Bryony, can you help my friend. He used all his energy to save me. Please, I didn't know who else to call for help.'

Bryony knelt down by Georgie, 'Yes I think I can, but please everyone step back, I need to act fast.' Bryony gestured for everyone to step back and held Georgie's hand with her left hand and placed her right hand onto the ground with her weather stone underneath it. Within seconds a black cloud appeared over their heads.

Rosie held Ellie's arms, 'Are you sure this is going to work?' she asked.

Bryony turned to them and said in nervous jest, 'He may explode, but I'm sure it'll be fine.' Before she'd even finished the sentence, a tiny bolt of lightning flew through her hat, down to her hand and into Georgie's hand. His body jolted and his bracelet shone bright orange. Bryony stood up and smiled.

'Easy,' she said.

With a groan Georgie opened his eyes and stretched. Seeing everyone looking down at him he smiled and jumped up to his feet.

'I knew I'd be all okay,' he smiled and turned to Bryony. 'You must be Bryony. Thank you for saving my life.'

'You're welcome,' she smiled, 'though I'm sorry but you will always have that mark of the lightning on your arm,' she looked down at his arm. Georgie followed her gaze and seeing a white mark on his arm, he smiled his broad grin. 'I love it! Do I have lightning powers now too?' Bryony shook her head. 'Unfortunately, no.'

'Never mind,' Georgie chuckled, 'this makes for a great talking point!'

Georgie, Bryony and Ellie felt elated but as they looked to the rest of the group, they realised they were the only ones.

'Let me get this straight,' Ayda said stepping towards the three of them. 'Ellie can conjure up weather conditions — but can't control them? Georgie, in trying to help Ellie control this nearly died, so a *Weather Witch* has had to come and save him using lightning and we're all OK about this?' Ayda shook her head in disbelief. 'It's not that I'm not grateful you saved my cousin, but who *are* you and how is Ellie going to be able to control the weather she's calling up when she doesn't know she's doing it in the first place?!' Everyone agreed that Ayda had a fair point.

Bryony stepped towards her with her hand out. 'I'm Bryony, pleased to meet you, pleased to meet you all,' she said, first shaking Ayda's hand and then waving to the others who were still stood at a safe distance. 'I have to be honest with you, I have no idea how Ellie can now call the weather — she showed no signs of being able to before coming here — something must have happened to trigger it.' Bryony scratched her head as she tried to figure out why this was happening.

'Ayda's right,' Birdie said 'How is Ellie going to manage this? It's dangerous for us all to continue on without making sure it's under control first.' Forest nodded in agreement.

'I have an idea,' Rosie said and got out her notebook. 'Finally, we get to see what you have been writing!' Birdie remarked.

'We need to get to the Forest of the Ancient Elders, they will have the answers we're looking for — I'm sure of it,' Rosie said confidently.

'But how do we get there?' Forest asked.

'I know the way,' Rosie replied. 'Follow me.'

Chapter 9

The Missing Chapter

The six Earth Witches and the one Weather Witch hadn't been walking long when they came to an opening into a dense wood. The ground here was thick with moss and ivy sparkling with the morning dew, and in front of the group stood a circle of large trees, full of leaves, all intertwined together by a thick vine. It was clear this was the Forest of the Ancient Elders. They walked towards the circle. As Ellie stepped forward, a dark cloud appeared to cover the centre of the circle and rumbled deeply.

Bryony looked at Ellie, then a bright bolt of lightning struck the central tree. The friends, startled, could all have sworn they heard a scream as it struck. Bryony shivered. 'This is not your usual thunder cloud, and I should know,' she stated.

Ellie glanced over to Rosie and saw she had tears in her eyes, she also saw that her seed ring was glowing brightly.

'Rosie,' Ellie said, understanding at once, 'she's your family isn't she — the young Earth Witch I mean. You want to free her.'

Rosie looked across to Ellie then down to the ground, as she nodded in reply to Ellie's questions. 'The lucky stone you gave me, it's not just a lucky stone is it? It's a weather stone isn't it? A broken weather stone. Is it hers?' All the pieces started to fit together.

'A fallen stone,' Bryony pondered, 'That would explain why you could suddenly call the weather — but as it's broken, you'd never be able to control it, it's just not possible.'

'A fallen stone, what do you mean by a "fallen stone"?' Ellie asked Bryony.

'When a Weather Witch becomes very old, they start to prepare for their final journey — it's very beautiful really — you can see them sparkling a couple of weeks before they begin their transition to becoming a star.'

While Ellie listened, she remembered how Elodie had sparkled the last time she saw her.

Bryony continued, 'When they do become a star, they have no more use for their weather stone so it stops glowing and falls to the earth. We call them fallen stones. They are very lucky things when they are found whole but can be quite destructive if broken.'

'She did find it whole, they broke it,' Rosie hissed turning her head towards the circle of trees ahead of them.

Ayda, beginning to understand, turned to Rosie and frowned. 'Why did you give Ellie the broken stone? How did you expect to free the Earth Witch from the enchantment? If you released her from the tree there would need to be a replacement, a sacrifice wouldn't there? Were you....?' She tailed off, shocked to realise the true reason Rosie had led them here.

'So, wait let me get this straight, you were leading me here as a sacrifice?!' Ellie accused Rosie, stunned by the revelation.

'Err, well, not really,' Rosie stuttered, looking down at the ground and anxiously squeezing her finger.

'She hesitated,' Bryony butted in, anxious to protect her friend, then continued off on a rant, 'I knew you shouldn't trust her, it's always the quiet ones. Something about being quiet and dangerous, what's the saying? I knew it. She was going to sacrifice you – who would do that in this day and age?! Well, I for one won't let that happen!' And with that Bryony raised her weather stone high in the sky but before she could call the lightning Rosie shouted as loud as she could –

'NO THAT IS NOT IT!! I WOULDN'T SACRIFICE ANOTHER WITCH BE THEY WEATHER OR EARTH! I AM NOT EVIL AND I AM NOT QUIET!' As Rosie shouted, the moss and ivy beneath her began to shrivel and die.

Both Ellie and Bryony stepped back away from Rosie.

'Well, *now* you're not quiet,' Bryony muttered under her breath.

Rosie looked down at the ground, 'Now look what you made me do,' she said to Bryony.

'Don't blame me that you got mad and made the ivy and moss shrivel!' Bryony retorted indignantly.

'I thought you were a healer?' Ellie said confused by the whole exchange, 'I mean, I saw you heal the golden leafed tree.'

'Yes, I am a healer,' Rosie said annoyed, 'but as I had tried to say before, all magic has opposites. So yes I *am* a healer, but I can also cause plants to die. It's not nice, I am ashamed of this side, but I do not let it rule me. Don't think of me as dangerous.'

'We don't,' Ellie said softly to Rosie reaching out her hand.

'I do,' Bryony disagreed, and kept her hands firmly in her pockets.

'Well, I don't. But please Rosie please tell me what your plan is?'

'Well,' Rosie began a little sheepishly, 'we need to get to the middle of the trees, the other half of the weather stone, or fallen stone as Bryony calls it, should be with the tree in the centre. You see she is my father's great, great aunty. When the ancient elders discovered she had found a weather stone and had the ability to call the weather, they got scared and broke it in half hoping to destroy its powers. She managed to retrieve both halves, giving one to her sister and fleeing with the other in the hope that when the elders stopped looking for her, the sisters would find each other and mend the stone; then they could learn to control both earth and weather powers. As you all know, she never managed to get away from them so the other half of the stone has been handed down in our family from generation to generation in the hope that one of us would be able to free her. I honestly think I have found the answer.' She paused, taking a deep breath before continuing. 'We need to reconnect the two halves of the stone and then, if my theory is correct, she should be released. They *all* should be released. There should be no reason for sacrifice or replacement, my plan is to free everyone.'

Bryony looked blankly, unconvinced. Ellie nodded slowly trying to take everything in. The others looked around at each other and then back to Rosie, who still had her eyes facing down to the ground.

'The Earth Witch Ancient Elders do not sound very nice,'
Bryony muttered.

'It sounds like they were scared,' Birdie said.

Chapter 10

Into the Circle of the Ancient Elders

Ayda walked close to the circle of trees and placed her hands on the ground. Using her powers, she could feel under the earth and through the tangled roots, finally reaching where the middle, seemingly dead, tree stood. Concentrating even harder she could feel a faint pulse from the other half of the stone.

'Rosie is right, the other half is with the tree. How do we get through them all though? They're tied tight together with vines?'

'I could try to reason with the trees?' Forest suggested. 'Maybe I could try to get the vines and branches to open slightly for us to get through?'

Forest stepped towards the circle of trees and placed one hand on the closest tree. Within seconds a vine came snapping up from the trunk and knocked Forest off his feet, slapping his face as he fell. He lay on the ground for a couple of seconds in shock.

'They are not happy,' he said. 'There's a lot of anger coming from them.' Birdie and Georgie helped Forest to his feet. The thunder cloud above the dead tree rumbled, releasing another bolt of lightning hard against its upturned branches.

The group began to walk around the circle of trees, trying to find some place where they could get through.

'Guys look,' Birdie suddenly said pointing to the base of the trees, 'do you see those symbols? They're a protection spell, this is why no one can enter. We need to break the spell. I could try to reverse it.'

Clearing her throat, Birdie began to say words the others had never heard before. She spoke clearly and loudly. Gradually, the symbols began to glow — it seemed to be working. Then, as the last word left her mouth, a strong pulse of light shot out from the trees — knocking all seven of them backwards and onto the ground. Dazed and sore, the group saw the thunder cloud growing bigger and bigger. Rain and thunder bolts started beating down into the centre of the circle.

Bryony got to feet first and mounted her broom. 'I'll try to calm the storm,' she said to the others as she flew high into the sky.

Vines and branches from the circle of trees flayed around and tried to catch her as she flew but Bryony was too fast and flew too high for them to even get close. Holding her weather stone aloft, she called, 'Lig an stoirm fúm!'* The lightning and rain eased slightly.

'I won't be able to hold this off for long!' she shouted down to the others. 'Whatever you're going to do please hurry!'

'We have to get through,' Ellie said.

'But how?' Forest asked.

'You have to use your negative power Rosie,' Birdie called across to Rosie, who was on the other side of the grove with Georgie. 'That's the only way we'll be able to penetrate the circle.'

Rosie looked in distress, terrified at the prospect. 'What if I lose control?' She turned to Georgie motioning to the grove that still clung tight together. 'I could kill the whole forest – I could hurt all of them.'

Georgie put his hand on hers and said calmly, 'I will help ground you, I will store your positive energy and if the negative

---

*   Lig an stoirm fúm (lig on stir-um foo-um) – Irish/Gaeilge for 'Storm be calm'/'Storm go from me' gets too much for you, I will release your positive energy back into you. You've got this Rosie...'

Rosie nodded, then reluctantly held onto one of the trees of the grove with both hands. Georgie's hands rested gently on her back. Their seeds began to glow. A stream of intense light spread from Rosie's hands into the trees of the grove. One by one they shone so brightly that everyone had to shelter their eyes. The tree Rosie held began to wither slightly, its branches started to recoil from the trees beside it. The tree shrieked as if in pain. Birdie and Ayda covered their ears. Forest fell to his knees covering his head with his arms in an attempt to stop the deafening sound. It was then that Ellie saw her chance and quickly crawled through the opening and into the middle of grove. As soon as Ellie got through the opening Rosie could no longer hold her power. She let go and as soon as she did the opening closed fast.

Ellie stood in the circle and looked around at the trees surrounding her. The opening she'd come through had vanished – she was trapped. Ellie could hear the voices of the ancient elders, calling her, warning her, taunting her it seemed – she covered her ears and turned away from them, though she couldn't block out their noise.

'You're destroying everything!' the voices shouted. 'You're hurting everyone!' The viciousness of the taunts almost took Ellie's breath away.

Ellie looked at the tree in the centre, where it stood bare from leaves, most of its branches broken. It looked like a dead tree – a snag – though Ellie couldn't help but think it also looked defiant standing there in the middle, its bare arms outstretched, reaching up to the skies.

Lightning struck the tree suddenly, sending a deafening crack through the circle, silencing the taunts for a brief moment. Startled by the sound, the half stone that Ellie had, fell from her hands. Ellie dropped to the ground desperately searching for it. Then the voices began to taunt again. 'You are worthless,' they spat. 'You are evil.' Ellie scrambled around on her knees feeling everywhere for the stone – then she saw a very slight glow. Yes! It was her half of the stone glowing ever so slightly as it lay at the base of the snag's trunk. Ellie quickly got to it and picked it up. She knew its other half must be close to have caused it to glow. She looked skywards and her heart sank as she saw, at the very top of the tree, tangled in the charred branches the flickering glow of the other half of the stone.

Ellie sat back onto her feet and thought. The voices seemed to be getting louder.

'How can I think with all that noise!'

Without thinking Ellie raised her hand and her acorn necklace began to glow brightly. The taunts immediately quietened and bounced back from her necklace into the tree's roots. Ellie realised what she had done and had an idea. She now focused all her energies around the trunk of the middle tree. It was working — the constant raging of insults was being blocked and the insults were bouncing back into the ancient elder trees. She noticed the trunk of the snag begin to look brighter — Ellie took a deep breath and started to climb as fast as she could — higher and higher.

Chapter 11

The Half Stones

Ellie was now so high she could see the tops of the ancient elder trees that were surrounding them. She hadn't quite realised how tall this tree actually was but knew she had to get to the other half of the fallen stone, so she continued to climb. The half stone in her pocket was glowing more and more the closer she got. She looked up and could just about see Bryony swirling above — holding back the lightning as much as she could. Ellie could see that Bryony was struggling so knew she had to power on.

Meanwhile, outside of the circle of trees the other Earth Witches could only look on feeling helpless. They watched the outside trees begin to shake slightly almost becoming smaller it seemed.

'The trees are growing quieter,' Forest said to the group. They looked at each other puzzled.

'Whatever Ellie is doing in there she must be doing it right!'
Birdie said as she walked around the trees inspecting each
one.

'I knew she would have the power,' Rosie said and clapped her
hands triumphantly. The others turned and looked at her. They
were not ready to rejoice just yet — they needed to know Ellie
was OK. Rosie saw this in their faces and looked down, letting
her hands drop to her sides.

Bryony was still way up high in the sky struggling to hold back
the unusual lightning. She briefly flew down to the rest of the
group.

'Any sign of Ellie yet?' she said out of breath slightly. The
others shook their heads. Bryony sighed and rubbed some
sweat from her forehead. 'It's the tree that's actually calling
the lightning, I mean, on purpose — it is purposely getting the
bolts to strike itself and they're not gentle bolts. These are
some of the strongest I've ever seen and I'm nearly finished
with my thunder and lightning training.'

Fear could be seen in Bryony's eyes and the thunder cloud on
the very tip of her hat was rumbling more so than ever, the
others could see the electrical pulses shooting inside it clearly.

Suddenly Georgie caught a glimpse of Ellie, over Bryony's
shoulder. She was on the very top branch of the dead tree.

'What is she doing?' Ayda muttered under her breath. Georgie heard. 'Don't worry — I know she's got this.' He held Ayda's hand. Bryony looked round shocked and quickly mounted her broom, flying up into the sky once more.

Ellie was now at the very top of the tree, she could see the half stone glowing brightly in the bare branches and was sure if she were to reach out, she could just about get it. She fumbled in her pocket and retrieved the half stone she had there. Steadying herself, she stretched out her arm and to her relief she felt a gentle magnetic pull, as the half stones struggled to come together. The pull became stronger, and Ellie couldn't stop her stone from slipping through her fingers. The two halves began to tumble to the ground, connecting together as they fell.

Ellie felt a mix of emotions as she saw the stones fuse, but before she could process anything a deafening, blinding bolt of lightning struck the tree cracking through its heart and throwing Ellie from its branches.

Georgie, Forest and the others saw the lightning and heard the loud crack as it struck. They watched helplessly as they saw Ellie falling from the top branch. She fell so fast she was soon out of their sight as she passed the tops of the ancient elder trees.

Rosie went pale. 'Nooo!' Georgie let go of Ayda's hand and tried to run through to the circle of trees, but it was still impassable. He ran round and around, looking up and down desperately trying to find a way he could squeeze through. Suddenly the tops of the trees all bowed forwards. Something was happening but what?

Inside the circle Ellie was still falling. Terrified, she closed her eyes, when, to her surprise she slowed down, bumping this way and that as though she was being held. Slowly she opened her eyes, first one and then the other, and she could see that the trees around her and the tree in the middle were extending their branches, linking them together and breaking her fall.

The lightning had stopped and a light warm rain had taken its place. Gently, bit by bit, the trees lowered Ellie to the ground.

Chapter 12

Fairy Circle

Almost as soon as Ellie touched the ground, she realised there was silence. At first, she thought the loud lightning strike that had caused her to fall may also have affected her hearing, but then she smelled a familiar sweetness in the air and knew the fairies must be near.

As Ellie slowly got to her feet and steadied herself, the Fairy Queen appeared in front of her — Ellie's broom magically appearing beside the Fairy Queen a few seconds after. Ellie glanced at the broom and then couldn't help but let out a long and despairing sigh, exhausted by everything.

'I haven't been able to bring you any of the items you requested,' she said.

The Fairy Queen started to speak with a softness Ellie was not expecting. 'Child, you have done so much more.'

She gestured around the circle in which they both stood. Ellie looked around. She noticed that the trees were all changing — the middle tree had even started to bloom a little.

The Fairy Queen continued, 'The items I requested were not needed. What was needed was for you to show me your true intentions. By not picking the last blue flower, not trapping the dragonfly and taking it from its home and by seeing the golden leaves are only golden when they are part of the tree, showed me how much you care for the natural world around you. I see now that you are a true Cailleach* child.' Ellie was familiar with this word; she had heard it in the land behind the clouds and was sure it meant witch. She smiled.

The Fairy Queen placed her hand on the tree beside them and Ellie saw the spirit of a young girl, which Ellie recognised from Georgie's story, appear holding the, now whole and glowing, fallen weather stone.

'You have done what many have failed to do before,' smiled the Fairy Queen, 'you have freed this tortured spirit.' The Fairy Queen handed Ellie her broom. Ellie, still trying to take it all in, accepted her broom and saw a new engraving sparkling on it. A feather.

---

*   Cailleach (ky-luck) — Irish/Gaeilge for witch/divine hag

'The broom is yours, the feather a gift from the Fae folk — take care of it — you never know, we may need to call on you again.' Ellie smiled broadly and admired the beautiful feather engraving.

The Fairy Queen turned and addressed the spirit in the tree, 'You are welcome to roam anywhere you choose — peace and freedom are yours.'

'I wish to guide and protect Ellie,' responded the spirit and with that she reached out and handed Ellie the fallen weather stone. As Ellie took the stone from her, the spirit of the girl followed and absorbed into it, creating a beautiful rainbow shimmer through the stone. Ellie held it tightly to her chest, her acorn necklace also shone brightly.

She looked to the Fairy Queen who had now turned her attention to the ancient elder trees surrounding them. She muttered some words. Ellie could just about make out the last sentence, 'Let this be forgiven but not forgotten.' The trees started to shake.

'What's happening to them?' Ellie asked, feeling a little scared.

The Fairy Queen calmly replied, 'You will soon see my child. You see, when fear and hate leave, the heart will bloom.' With those final words the Fairy Queen faded, and the sweet smell was gone. Ellie could hear the birds and feel the breeze again.

One by one the Ancient Elder trees began to vanish — a circle of mushrooms taking their place. The tree Ellie stood beside was now in full bloom and she noticed a few flowers were starting to appear around the circle.

'It can take a while for hate to leave,' Ellie thought to herself as she started to walk out of the circle. She looked up and smiled as she saw her friends all looking at her with such relief and, as soon as she stepped out of the circle, they ran and hugged her.

Ellie turned to Rosie. 'I feel like you should have this,' she said handing her the complete Weather Stone. Rosie shook her head folding Ellie's fingers over the stone and pushing it back to her.

'No, not at all, you must never give away a gifted Weather Stone,' Rosie said. 'You have the weather powers — I don't — it belongs with you. You freed my great aunty that is more than enough for me.'

It felt like ages since Ellie had been home. She was tired and really wanted to tell her mother all that had happened and everything she had learned. Rosie shared the notes from her book with Ellie and the others — it told of their big adventure and also her thoughts about her new friends. (There were some gasps but also lots of laughter.) She had even kept a page especially about Bryony.

Sitting round the campfire the little band of Earth Witches quietly reflected on their journey together. 'We make a good team,' Birdie said, and everyone nodded in agreement. 'The best coven of Earth and Weather Witches,' she added with a smile. It had been fun — scary at times — but they were all ready to go home.

Chapter 13

A Fallen Stone

As dusk began to creep in, the friends heard a call from the skies. They looked up and could see Amara the mynah bird returning to the group. 'I bring news, important news,' she chirped and raised her claw which had a note attached to it. Georgie carefully took and read the note. He turned to Bryony and handed it to her. Bryony sighed sadly. 'We must get back Ellie,' she said. 'Why? Is everything OK?' Ellie quizzed, concerned at Bryony's tone. 'It's Elodie, I can sense she's changing.' Ellie knew exactly what Bryony meant and said her final goodbyes to everyone. Bryony and Ellie then mounted their brooms and flew as fast as they could.

The skies were calm, the flight was smooth, yet they still had a long way ahead of them. Ellie looked up to the stars. Bryony flew to her side. 'You're getting quite good at this whole flying thing and with all your new-found powers, you must be some kind of super witch right?' she teased. Ellie smiled — she knew what Bryony was doing — she was trying to distract her from her thoughts.

'You never know,' Ellie replied in a like manner, 'I may even have some síoga* powers too!' As Ellie spoke, she passed her hand lightly over the feather engraving on her broom that the fairies had gifted her. It sparkled a little.

Ellie and Bryony looked at each other as they both felt a pulsing of energy entering the sky, sparkling lights followed close behind. Purples and greens lit up the sky for just a second and then the lights were gone, the night sky was dark again, just the moon and the stars glowing above. However, this time, they both noticed that one star stood out in particular. It seemed to shine brighter than the others.

'We're too late,' Ellie called to Bryony pointing to the new star and holding back tears. Bryony looked at the star and smiled. 'Maybe too late to say goodbye but look how she's shining. She's brighter than all the other stars — she always will be to her friends and family. You can talk to her star if it makes you feel better. Don't be too upset Ellie she'll always be with us, for witches never truly leave.'

Ellie liked this idea; she'd never thought about life and death like this before. It comforted her to know Elodie was shining on them, she could feel she was with them on their journey home.

The star shone brightly.

---

*   Síoga (she-oh-ga) — Irish/Gaeilge for fairies

Meanwhile, somewhere far, far away a grey stone, with a hole right through the middle fell from the sky and landed gently onto a pebble beach finding its place — a fallen stone waiting to be found. In the distance the waves were lightly lapping the shore.

Glossary

'spéir ceobhránach tosnaigh!' (spare keo-vrawn-uck tus-nig) — Irish/Gaeilge for 'foggy/misty skies!'

Síoga (she-oh-ga) — Irish/Gaeilge for fairies

'Beir greim ar do chrann scuaibe' (Bear grime air duh crown scuba) — Irish/Gaeilge for 'Hold on to your broom/brushes'

Cailleach (Ky-luck) — Irish/Gaeilge for witch/divine hag

'Lig an stoirm fúm!' (lig on stir-um foo-um) — Irish/Gaeilge for 'Storm be calm/storm go from me!'

Phoenix Sequoia Seeds — Based on the Giant Sequoia seeds that need fire to grow

Always Remember the Power of Words

Words can be powerful, magical things. They can create and they can heal but be careful as they can also hurt and harm. Remember to always use kind and positive words to yourself and others.

We all have the magic power of words —
let's use them wisely!

More from

child's
eye

Miss Polly and the Crocodile

Felicia Thomas

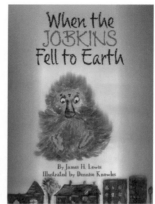

When the JOBKINS Fell to Earth

By James H. Lewis
Illustrated by Dennise Knowles

Lockdown Lit

Antie Corona

Unlocked minds – a collection of children's short stories written during the COVID-19 pandemic

Edited by Steven Lane

Great Uncle Stanley

By Katherine Lane
Illustrations by Tom Wells

Written by Steve Roberts
Illustrated by Lisa Dunkley

DUG
When grandfathers GO BAD

Bryony Fairview: Weather Witch

by Rebecca Burke
Illustrated by Chris Burke